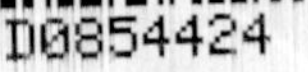

This book belongs to:

WINNIE THE POOH

RABBIT

CHRISTOPHER ROBIN

EEYORE

STARRING

OWL

KANGA & ROO

This is a Parragon book
First published in 2006

Parragon
Queen Street House
4 Queen Street
Bath, BA1 1HE, UK

ISBN 978-1-4054-8323-0
Printed in China

Based on the "Winnie the Pooh" works by A.A. Milne and E.H. Shepard.

The Honey Tree

p

Winnie the Pooh sat on the log outside his little house. It was the finest autumn day anyone could remember. There wasn't a breath of wind and the smoke from Pooh's fire drifted straight up into the sky.

Everything was perfect except for one thing – Pooh had run out of honey! Pooh sighed as he looked at all the empty honey pots scattered around him.

Pooh decided to do his exercises to take his mind off his rumbly tummy. He was attempting to touch his toes when he heard a buzzing sound.

"That buzzing sound means something," Pooh said thoughtfully. "Buzzing means bees and where there are bees there's usually honey!"

Pooh followed the bee until he came to the foot of a very tall tree. He looked up and saw the bee fly into a hole.

"I don't suppose the bees would mind if I borrowed a little honey," said Pooh as he began to climb the tree.

Pooh climbed all the way up to the honey-bee hole.

As Pooh leaned closer to the hole, the little branch he was clinging to began to bend. The more he leaned the more it bent, until he could almost reach the honey. He leaned just a little bit further when ... CRACK! The branch snapped.

Pooh bounced from branch to branch, then BUMP! He landed headfirst in a bush!

Pooh rubbed his sore head so hard that he came up with an idea. "Perhaps Christopher Robin will be able to help me reach the honey."

Christopher Robin and Kanga were busy sorting out his old toys.

"Hello!" Pooh called. Then he spotted a blue balloon. "That's just the thing!" he said. "Could I borrow that balloon so I can get some honey?"

"Honey?" said Christopher Robin. "From a balloon?"

"I shall float up to the bee hole," explained Pooh. "The bees will think I'm a cloud!"

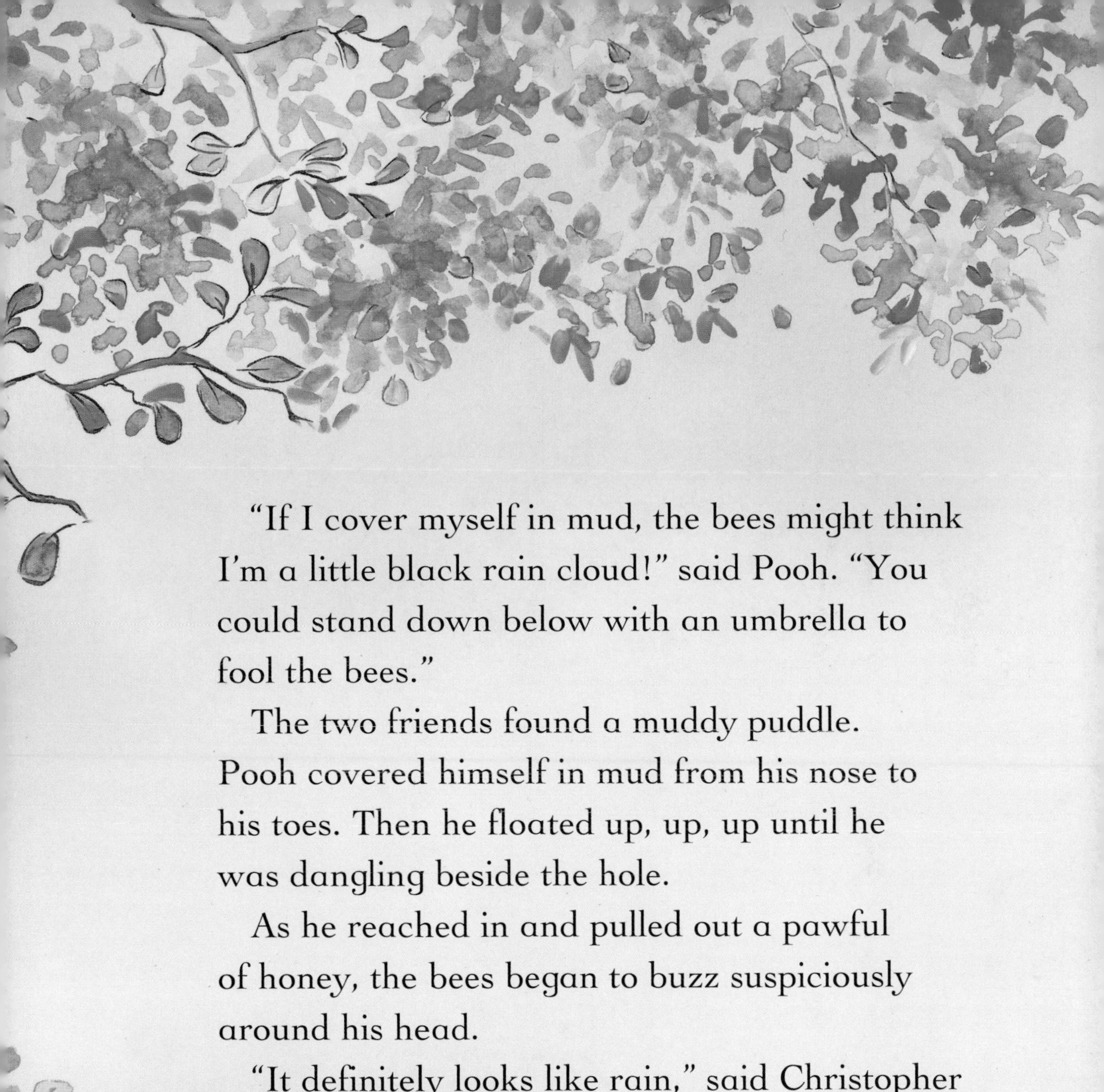

"If I cover myself in mud, the bees might think I'm a little black rain cloud!" said Pooh. "You could stand down below with an umbrella to fool the bees."

The two friends found a muddy puddle. Pooh covered himself in mud from his nose to his toes. Then he floated up, up, up until he was dangling beside the hole.

As he reached in and pulled out a pawful of honey, the bees began to buzz suspiciously around his head.

"It definitely looks like rain," said Christopher Robin, pacing back and forth with his umbrella.

The honey-bee tree fell silent. Then a rumble began deep in the hole, which turned into an angry buzz-buzz-BUZZ!

Just at that moment, the balloon began to lose air. Pooh clung on tightly as the balloon swooshed along, followed by a swarm of angry bees.

"Hang on!" cried Christopher Robin.

Pooh landed in a puddle with a PLOP! Christopher Robin jumped in after him and used his umbrella to hide them from the bees.

"It all comes from liking honey so much!" said Pooh.

By then it was lunchtime and Pooh was hungrier than ever, so he sat down to think. First of all he thought about honey and then he thought about his friend Rabbit. Rabbit always had plenty of honey, so Pooh hurried over to his house.

"Hello, Rabbit!" called Pooh.

"Uh... er... come in, Pooh," said Rabbit cautiously.

Although Rabbit was one of Pooh's best friends, he knew what happened when Pooh visited at lunchtime.

"I see you were just about to have a snack," said Pooh, spotting the jars of honey in Rabbit's arms. "Would you mind if I joined you?"

"Why not?" said Rabbit with a sigh.

At first, Pooh sampled each honey pot one at a time. However, Rabbit had such delicious honey that Pooh couldn't help himself! He ate and ate and ate.

Rabbit's ears drooped lower as the empty honey pots piled up around Pooh. Finally, there was none left.

Pooh rose slowly from the table. "Goodbye, Rabbit," he said in a rather sticky voice.

However, he couldn't fit through the door! His rather full middle was stuck in the middle! Rabbit pushed and pushed but Pooh would not budge.

"Bother!" said Pooh, waggling his legs. "It all comes from not having a big enough front door."

"Nonsense!" said Rabbit sharply. "It all comes from eating too much!" And he hurried out of his back door to fetch Christopher Robin.

"Silly old bear," said Christopher Robin when he returned with an anxious-looking Rabbit. He took hold of Pooh's paws and pulled and pulled, but Pooh was stuck tight.

"We'll just have to wait for you to get thin!" said Christopher Robin.

So they all waited. Christopher Robin read stories to Pooh. Owl flew down to lecture Pooh on the dangers of eating too much. Kanga even hopped by with a handkerchief to protect Pooh's head from the hot sun.

RABBIT'S
HOWSE

That night, Pooh was thinking how hungry he was when Gopher popped up to eat his snack.

"Is that honey in your lunch box?" asked Pooh.

"Why yes," replied Gopher. "Would you like some?"

Inside his house, Rabbit thought he had heard someone offering Pooh honey. Honey that would make him fatter and keep him stuck in the front door forever!

"Stop, stop, stop!" Rabbit cried. He rushed out of his back door and grabbed the honey pot from Pooh's paws. "Not a bite! Not a lick! Not a drop!"

Then Rabbit stuck a sign in front of Pooh.

RABBIT'S
HOWSE

The next morning, Rabbit was busy tidying up when he leaned against Pooh's bottom to rest. Pooh moved!

"Hooray! He budged!" Rabbit cried. "He bidged! He badged! He boodged!" He ran off to fetch Christopher Robin.

Before long, all of Pooh's friends arrived to help free Pooh. Christopher Robin grabbed Pooh's paws. Kanga grabbed Christopher Robin and Eeyore grabbed Kanga. They all pulled as hard as they could.

Meanwhile, Rabbit ran into his house. He backed up in his living room as far as he could, then he ran across the floor at top speed. He threw himself at Pooh's bottom and pushed with all his might.

POP! Pooh flew out of the hole and sailed over the grassy place in front of Rabbit's house.

"Watch out, Pooh!" cried Kanga.

Pooh was heading straight for another honey tree! He landed headfirst in the hole.

BUZZZZ! Pooh's sudden appearance startled the bees and they swarmed off over the treetops.

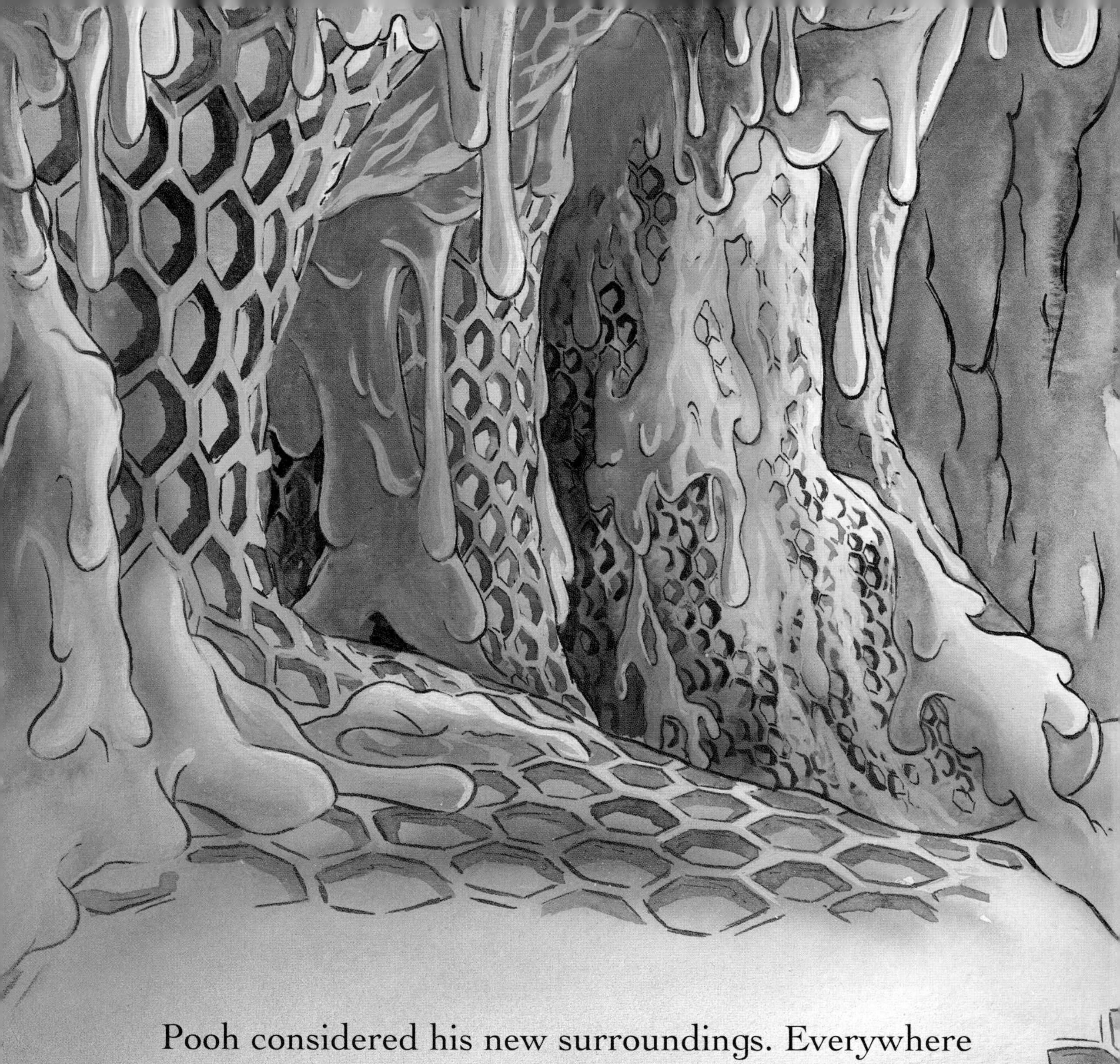

Pooh considered his new surroundings. Everywhere he looked, he saw delightful, mouth-watering honey.

"Don't worry, Pooh!" Christopher Robin cried, "we'll soon have you out of there!"

"Thank you!" called Pooh, between mouthfuls of warm, delicious honey. "But I'm not in any hurry!"